Sonny's Secret

YOUNG YEARLING BOOKS YOU WILL ENJOY:

The Pee Wee Scout books by Judy Delton

COOKIES AND CRUTCHES
CAMP GHOST-AWAY
LUCKY DOG DAYS
BLUE SKIES, FRENCH FRIES
GRUMPY PUMPKINS
PEANUT-BUTTER PILGRIMS
A PEE WEE CHRISTMAS
THAT MUSHY STUFF
SPRING SPROUTS
THE POOPED TROOP
THE PEE WEE JUBILEE
BAD, BAD BUNNIES
ROSY NOSES, FREEZING TOES

YEARLING BOOKS/YOUNG YEARLINGS/YEARLING CLASSICS are designed especially to entertain and enlighten young people. Patricia Reilly Giff, consultant to this series, received her bachelor's degree from Marymount College and a master's degree in history from St. John's University. She holds a Professional Diploma in Reading and a Doctorate of Humane Letters from Hofstra University. She was a teacher and reading consultant for many years, and is the author of numerous books for young readers.

For a complete listing of all Yearling titles, write to
Dell Readers Service, P.O. Box 1045,
South Holland, IL 60473.

Sonny's Secret

JUDY DELTON

Illustrated by Alan Tiegreen

A YOUNG YEARLING BOOK

For Baby Mark
With thanks to his mother

Published by
Dell Publishing
a division of
Bantam Doubleday Dell Publishing Group, Inc.
1540 Broadway
New York, New York 10036

ISBN: 0-440-40429-0

Printed in the United States of America

July 1991

10 9 8 7 6 5 4 3 2

CWO

Contents

CHAPTER 1

Surprise!

"I know something you don't know," sang Sonny Betz. All the Pee Wee Scouts were getting on the bus to go to their meeting. It was Tuesday. Tuesday was their meeting day. They met at the home of their leader, Mrs. Peters.

"Ho, I'll bet," said Roger White. "I know everything you know, Betz."

"You don't know this," said Sonny.

"You're getting a new pet," said Molly Duff.

Sonny shook his head.

"New shoes," said Tim Noon. Tim liked

new shoes. He didn't get new clothes very often.

"Big deal," scoffed Rachel Meyers. "New shoes aren't news."

Rachel had all kinds of shoes.

Black ones and white ones.

Red ones and blue ones.

She even had dancing shoes. Tap shoes and little pink satin ballet shoes.

"My news isn't shoes," said Sonny.

"Tell us!" shouted Tracy Barnes. She jumped up and down in the bus aisle. "It's not nice to keep secrets."

Sonny was enjoying all the attention. He put his fingers to his lips and turned a make-believe key and threw it away. "I know and you don't," he said. "I'm not telling."

Mary Beth Kelly stamped her foot. "Sonny Betz, you tell us this second," she said.

Sonny just sat with his arms folded.

The other Scouts began to lose interest.

Kevin Moe took out his penknife and studied it. The Scouts watched him open and shut the little blade.

"Can I do it?" asked Kenny Baker.

Kenny and Patty Baker were twins.

"All right!" shouted Sonny. "I'll tell one of you."

"Me, me, me!" screamed Lisa Ronning. All of the Scouts swarmed around Sonny again.

Sonny took a long time choosing someone to tell. He pointed his finger at one, then another.

"I'll tell . . . you!" he said finally.

His finger stopped at Roger.

"I don't want to know," said Roger. "I don't care what your dumb secret is."

Sonny pointed to Molly. He put his mouth to her ear. He was just about to whisper something.

4

Suddenly, Rachel said, "I'll bet your mom is getting married."

"How did you know?" Sonny said, looking upset.

"I just guessed," said Rachel. "Your mom has been going out with the fire chief ever since we went to the fire station. People get married when they go out. Sometimes."

"Who cares?" said Roger.

Molly felt sorry for Sonny. This was big news for him. Sonny would have a father! He was sort of a mama's boy. A baby. It would be good for Sonny to have a father.

"That's wonderful!" said Molly warmly.

"Well, they're engaged," said Sonny. "He's getting her this great big diamond ring. It costs a lot."

The girls asked some questions.

The boys went back to taking turns opening Kevin's penknife.

"Here we are," called the bus driver. "All out for Mrs. Peters's!"

The Pee Wees tumbled out of the bus. Mrs. Peters was waiting at the door. She was waving and smiling. Tiny and Lucky were barking. Tiny was Mrs. Peters's dog. Lucky was Troop 23's mascot. They liked Tuesdays too.

"Hurry!" called their leader. "We have a lot of things to do today."

Everyone followed Mrs. Peters through the house and down into the basement. They all took their places around a big table. They said their Pee Wee Scout pledge and sang their Pee Wee Scout song.

Then Mrs. Peters asked about good deeds.

"I ordered Chinese food from the take-out place," said Rachel, with a toss of her head.

"What kind of a good deed is that?" said Roger. "It would be a better good deed if you cooked it."

"I'm a big help to my mother, smarty-pants," said Rachel. "I'd like to see you cook Chinese food."

Rachel began to pout. Mrs. Peters put her hand up. "Whether you cook it or order it, I'm sure it is a big help to your mother," she said.

Rachel stuck out her tongue at Roger.

Other hands were waving with good deeds to report.

"I sewed this button on my sweater when it fell off," said Lisa. She held up her sweater to show the button.

"How come the thread is green?" asked Tracy. "The other ones are sewn on with red thread."

"I didn't have any red," said Lisa. "It's sewed on tight, that's the important thing."

The Scouts clapped for Lisa's tight button.

Some more Scouts told about good deeds.

"I didn't run over anthills with my bike," said Tim.

"I ate my whole lunch at school," said Kenny. "Even though I hate pears. I didn't throw anything out."

"I took some cough medicine and it tasted icky," said Mary Beth.

"How's that a good deed?" said Kevin. "A good deed to yourself!"

"My dad said coughing makes people nervous," said Mary Beth. "So it was a good deed."

"And now," said Mrs. Peters, "we'll go on to other things. I have lots of news today. News about a new badge we are all going to earn. And good news about some-one we all know."

The Pee Wees looked around the table.

Oh, no, thought Molly. More secrets. I hope we don't have to guess, she said to herself.

CHAPTER 2

Bad Manners to Burp

"**F**irst, I'll tell you the wonderful news about someone in this very room," said Mrs. Peters.

"Me?" said Roger.

"It's Sonny," said Kevin. "He's going to get a dad."

Mrs. Peters frowned.

Kevin blabbed her good news, thought Molly.

But Mrs. Peters plunged ahead as if she had not heard Kevin. "We have a wedding coming up in our group!" she said.

"We're too young to get married, Mrs. Peters," said Tracy.

Mrs. Peters laughed. "You are," she said, "but not Sonny's mother. Mrs. Betz is engaged to be married to Larry, the fire chief, very soon."

Sonny stood up at the table, knocking down his chair. He bowed and smiled.

"Cheese Louise," said Tim. "We know that already." Sonny's mother was named Louise.

Mrs. Peters began to clap softly, and motioned the Scouts to applaud also. A few hands clapped weakly.

"Since Mrs. Betz is our assistant troop leader, and a very good friend," Mrs. Peters went on, "she would like all of the Pee Wees to be in the wedding."

"Don't you mean *at* the wedding, Mrs. Peters?" said Mary Beth.

"No, I mean *in* the wedding," their leader

11

replied. "She has asked all of Pee Wee Scout Troop 23 to be part of the wedding party, and to walk down the aisle, scattering peony petals along the way."

"I was in my cousin's wedding," said Rachel. "So I know what to do already."

"Good, Rachel, then you can help us," said Mrs. Peters.

It was just like Rachel to know all about weddings, thought Molly. She knew all about everything.

"I'm going to be the ring bear," said Sonny proudly.

"What's a ring bear?" asked Lisa.

"A ring *bearer*," said Mrs. Peters, "is the person who carries the wedding ring down the aisle.

"The important thing about a wedding," said Mrs. Peters, "is that we have to have very good manners."

The Scouts groaned. They did not like good manners.

"And that brings me to my second piece of good news," Mrs. Peters went on. "We are going to earn a brand-new badge this month."

"Yeah!" shouted all of the Pee Wees. They loved badges.

Badges were colorful.

Red, blue, green, yellow.

Badges were fun.

Molly already had many badges.

A first-aid badge.

A help-a-pet badge.

A camping badge.

A skating badge.

A team-spirit badge.

Even a fitness badge.

The Pee Wees had to work hard to get badges. But it was worth it to sew a new one on your shirt along with all the others.

"What's the new badge?" the Scouts shouted, jumping up and down.

Lucky and Tiny barked at all the excitement. Arf! Arf!

"The new badge," said Mrs. Peters, "is a good-manners badge."

"Rat's knees," said Molly in disgust.

"I have good manners every day," said Rachel. "I don't need a badge for saying 'please' and 'thank you.'"

"There is more to good manners than please and thank you," said Mrs. Peters.

The Scouts were getting restless. Molly was wondering if Mrs. Peters had made a treat for them this afternoon. She felt hungry. She wondered if baby Nick was going to wake up from his nap and come and join them. Molly loved Mrs. Peters's baby. He had one tooth and he made noises that sounded like "Mama" and "Daddy."

Mrs. Peters clapped her hands. "Good manners can be fun," she said, trying to get their attention back.

"Manners are for girls," said Roger. "For sissies."

Mrs. Peters's face grew red. She looked like she might stomp her foot and yell at

Roger. But Mrs. Peters calmed down. "Manners are for civilized people, Roger," she said. "Let's make a list of things that are good manners. And a list of bad manners too."

She picked up a piece of chalk and set up a little chalkboard on the table. Hands began to wave.

"It's bad manners to burp," shouted Roger, trying to redeem himself.

The boys began to burp loudly. All the Pee Wees laughed.

"We will put that under bad manners, Roger—although it isn't bad manners, exactly, if it is done quietly. It is bad manners, though, to laugh loudly when someone burps."

"It's bad manners to whistle at the table," said Kenny Baker. "When you're eating."

Mrs. Peters wrote that under BAD MANNERS.

"Hitting kids is bad manners," said Tim.

"It certainly is," Mrs. Peters agreed. "Now, what about good manners? That is what we want to practice."

"Don't pick up your soup bowl and drink from it," said Lisa.

"Eat soup quietly with a spoon," wrote Mrs. Peters under GOOD MANNERS. "Good, Lisa," she said.

Mrs. Peters put down the chalk and picked up a big piece of paper. She unfolded it. It was a big poster. She held it up.

"This might help," she said.

At the top it said LET'S MIND OUR MANNERS and underneath were pictures of people doing just that.

There was a boy with a napkin on his lap.

Another boy was opening a door for an old lady.

A little curly-headed girl gave her bus seat to a man with a cane.

17

A lady took the smallest piece of cake on a plate.

Mrs. Peters explained all the pictures. "What do you notice about all of these people?" she asked.

"They're funny," said Mary Beth.

"They are all white," said Lisa, who was black.

"They dress weird," said Kevin.

Mrs. Peters shook her head. "They are all smiling!" she said. "It is very, very good manners to have a smile on your face, instead of walking around all grumpy and frowning."

Mrs. Peters made a grumpy face. Then she gave a big smile.

"Which one is more pleasant to see?" she asked.

"A smile!" shouted all the Pee Wee Scouts together.

"A smile is good manners," Mrs. Peters

said. "No one wants to see people who are mean and grumpy.

"I want you all to keep a manners diary this month. Every time you see someone with good manners, write down what they have done. Write down things you do to show good manners. We will see who has the longest list of good manners when it comes time for badges.

"The wedding will be the final wrap-up of our good manners month. It will be our chance to show all the good manners that we have learned. Later we will talk about wedding etiquette and how to behave during the ceremony."

"When can we eat?" asked Roger.

"Now," said Mrs. Peters. "We will have some chocolate-chip cookies for our treat."

The Pee Wee Scouts cheered.

Mrs. Peters brought the cookies down from the kitchen upstairs. Then she brought down baby Nick. The Scouts played with the baby. Then they played one game of charades, and before long it was time to sing the Pee Wee Scout song and leave for home.

"See you next week!" called Mrs. Peters. "Remember to keep your diary and look for ways you can show good manners to others."

Outside, Mrs. Betz and Larry were there to pick up Sonny in the car.

"They're in love," whispered Mary Beth to Molly, when they saw the car. Mary Beth was Molly's best friend. "See how they look at each other. I'll bet they kiss each other on the mouth a lot."

It was hard to picture Mrs. Betz kissing Larry on the mouth. But grown-ups could be mushy. Molly knew that. The important thing was that Sonny would have a father. And maybe then he would grow up too.

CHAPTER 3

Please and Thank you

The next day, after school, Molly bought a new notebook and a new pencil. On the front she wrote MANNERS DIARY. Then she called Mary Beth. "Let's go look for good manners," she said.

Mary Beth came over to Molly's house. She was carrying a notebook too. "My mom said I have to use my old spelling notebook," she said.

The girls each wrote GOOD MANNERS at the top of one page.

21

They wrote BAD MANNERS at the top of another page.

Then they started down the street together. At the corner they waited for a car to pass. The car slowed down and let them cross. Molly opened her notebook and turned to the page that said GOOD MANNERS.

"Three-thirty P.M.," she wrote. "A lady slowed down in her car to let us cross the street."

Mary Beth wrote it down too.

In the next block, a woman was coming toward them. She had a poodle on a leash. She had her arms full of groceries. The woman was in the middle of the sidewalk. There wasn't much room for the girls to pass. They had to walk around her, on the grass.

Molly turned to BAD MANNERS and wrote down, "Three thirty-five. Lady hogged the sidewalk."

"May we help you carry your groceries?" said Mary Beth politely to the woman with bad manners.

"Why, how kind you are," the lady replied.

The girls took the big bags of groceries. They were heavy. It was a long way to the woman's house. The poodle nipped at their heels as they walked.

Finally they got there and the lady gave them each a cookie. "You have wonderful manners," she said.

"We know," said Mary Beth. "We are Pee Wee Scouts."

When they got outside, the girls wrote, "Carried groceries home for a lady," under GOOD MANNERS.

"We've got a lot!" said Molly. "We might fill our notebooks by next Tuesday."

"Let's sit in front of the minimall," said Mary Beth. "Lots of people go by there. I'll bet some of them have manners."

The girls plopped down on a bench and chewed on their pencils.

Rachel came by with her mother. She held a big package from a dress shop. "I'm going to a birthday party," she said. "At the Brewsters'."

The Brewsters were rich. They had a pool inside their house. They swam in it in the middle of winter.

"Big deal," said Molly, when they were gone.

"It's bad manners to brag," said Mary Beth.

Both girls wrote "Rachel bragged" in their notebooks.

For a while no one came along with any manners. Good ones or bad ones. Then a girl stopped in front of a store window and combed her hair. Her friend blew bubbles with her bubble gum.

"It's bad manners to comb your hair in public," whispered Molly. "And to blow bubbles."

They wrote it down.

A little boy sat on the bench next to them.

His nose was running. He sniffed. Then he wiped his nose on his sleeve.

The girls wrote it down.

Their notebooks were filling up fast.

"There's Kenny!" shouted Molly.

Sure enough, Kenny was helping a man with a cane to cross the street.

"I've got twenty-five manners!" he called to them. "Patty's got fifteen."

Molly groaned. They would have to work harder to beat the twins.

But when the girls looked at Kenny's notebook, they saw a long list of the times he said "Please" and "Thank you."

"You get more if you do the manners yourself," he said. "We said 'Excuse me' and 'Have a nice day' a lot. And we smile at people."

"You can't write it down every time you smile at someone," scoffed Mary Beth.

"Yes, you can," said Kenny. "Mrs. Peters said."

Good manners was getting easier. No wonder the Baker twins had so many on their list!

Pretty soon Lisa and Kevin came by. They sat down on the bench next to the other Pee Wees. Everyone shoved over. It was getting crowded on the bench.

The sun felt warm on Molly's head. Molly began to daydream. It was a good time for a wedding, she thought. Grass would come up. Flowers would bloom. The Pee Wees would be all dressed up. Molly couldn't wait. She had never been in a wedding before.

Suddenly she remembered something. At weddings people took pictures. They put them in shiny white albums. Molly would be in that album. All the Pee Wees would be in the Stones' wedding album forever.

She turned to tell Mary Beth that news, but Mary Beth was arguing with Lisa.

"That's a lie," said Mary Beth.

"It is not," said Lisa. "My mom told me."

"Told you what?" asked Molly, forgetting the wedding pictures.

"Lisa says, if you talk with your mouth full, your teeth will fall out," said Mary Beth.

"Talk and chew, no teeth for you," sang Lisa.

Molly felt a chill go down her back, even though they were sitting in the sun. Was Lisa right? Was her mother reliable? Molly believed what her own mother and father said. Parents usually told the truth.

What if her teeth really did fall out? Clunk, clunk, clunk. Everyone would laugh and point at her. She wouldn't be able to chew at all. She'd have to eat baby food, like Mary Beth's little sister.

"I have to go home," said Kenny, jumping up. "It's almost supper time."

Molly didn't feel hungry at all.

CHAPTER 4

Good-bye, Teeth

The Pee Wees started toward home.

Mary Beth turned at the corner and Molly ran home. Her mother and father were waiting at the dinner table.

"You're late," said her dad, giving her a hug. "I was getting hungry."

Molly didn't feel hungry. She kept feeling her teeth with her tongue. She kept hearing them all drop out of her mouth.

Clunk, clunk, clunk.

How tight were they in there?

She had to remember never to talk and

chew. Probably the best way was not to eat or chew at all.

"I'm not hungry," she said to her parents.

"Pork chops are your favorite," said her mother. "And I made mashed potatoes and gravy."

Molly ate a little bit. She hoped her father didn't ask a question about school. She only opened her mouth a little bit to slide the meat in. Then she clamped it shut and didn't open it until she swallowed.

"Do you want some applesauce?" asked her mother.

Was this a trick? Was her mother trying to trick her into a bad manner? Molly shook her head.

"It's bad manners to shake your head, Molly," said her dad. "You should say 'No, thank you,' if you don't want any."

Was everything a bad manner? She had

to pick one. Was it a worse bad manner to talk and eat, or to shake her head? At least Lisa didn't say what happened if you shook your head instead of saying "No, thank you."

Finally Molly excused herself and ran to her room. She opened her notebook and wrote down, "Shook my head instead of saying 'No, thank you,'" under BAD MAN-NERS.

Then she turned to the back of the note-book and wrote a message to herself. "Never never never talk with food in my mouth."

Then she drew a picture of a row of teeth at the bottom. The teeth were on the floor. They weren't in her mouth. Beside them, she drew a picture of Lisa with the words, "I told you so," in a balloon coming out of her mouth.

The next morning Mary Beth said, "I'm going over to Tracy's after school."

"Can you come too?" Tracy asked Molly. "We can find some more good manners."

"I'll ask my mom," said Molly.

All day long Molly kept saying the rhyme over and over to herself. She didn't want to forget it for one minute. It was too risky. "Talk and chew, no teeth for you," she said under her breath.

"Molly," said her teacher. "I asked you to spell 'wagon.'"

Molly spelled it. She spelled it wrong.

In math class, she said four and four were six instead of eight.

In geography, she couldn't find the north pole.

At recess she played the Farmer in the Dell with her classmates. She forgot all about the silly rhyme until Lisa said, "Look at that boy who is the cheese."

Molly looked. He was smiling even though he wasn't a Pee Wee Scout. And when he smiled, Molly could see that he had no teeth in his mouth!

"I'll bet he talked and chewed at the same time," said Lisa.

Lisa clapped and sang, "The cheese stands alone," with the rest of the group. But Molly couldn't sing. Here was proof that Lisa's mother was right! Molly had lost one baby tooth, but a new one had come in. This boy didn't seem to have a single tooth in his mouth. New or old.

Molly thought about the boy who was the cheese all day long.

After school, Molly stopped at her own house to get permission to go to Tracy's.

"Be home for dinner," said her mother.

The girls played with Tracy's dolls in her room. Then they went out to her garage and watched her brother, Mike, build a go-cart out of orange crates. He used old bicycle wheels to make it roll.

The girls had such a good time they forgot all about manners. They rode in the go-cart when it was finished.

Up and down the sidewalk.

In and out of the driveway.

Their hair blew in the breeze as they flew along in the cart.

"It's like a car!" shouted Mary Beth. "It's like having your very own car!"

Tracy's brother nailed on an old license plate.

He put on a running board.

Then he put on an old horn from a tricycle that was too old and rusty to ride.

"Honk, honk!" they all sang as they drove down the street. "Get out of our way!"

"I wish this thing had an engine," said Mike.

"Then we could get gas and go faster," said Tracy.

Tracy's mother came out in the yard and gave them candy bars. The girls thanked her, and unwrapped them. Molly stuffed

half of the bar into her mouth. She was thinking of the go-cart.

"We could take the engine out of my dad's old lawn mower in our basement!" she shouted. "He doesn't use it anymore."

Three peanuts jumped out of Molly's mouth and onto the sidewalk as she talked. "Yikes!" she said out loud.

Would her teeth be next?

CHAPTER 5

An Easy Mistake

Molly started to run home. She ran and ran without stopping until she got to her house.

"What's the rush?" called her mother, as Molly ran through the kitchen and upstairs to her room. Molly didn't answer.

She slammed the door to her room and threw herself on her bed. She moved her tongue around in her mouth. They were still there. There were no empty spots. Not yet.

When her mother called her for supper, she went down. She had better eat while she still could chew. Pretty soon she'd be eating baby food and applesauce.

After she dried the supper dishes, she looked in the mirror in the bathroom. She counted every tooth. None missing so far. But would she have to spend her life counting her teeth every hour? She decided to brush her teeth for the last time. She remembered how she used to argue with her mom about brushing them. If only her teeth could be saved, she wouldn't have to be reminded to brush them ever again.

When Molly brushed her teeth, she felt one move. She put her finger on it. Sure enough, it was loose! The tooth wiggled back and forth when she touched it.

"Molly," her mother called up the steps. "Mary Beth is here."

Molly went out in the yard. Mary Beth was sitting on the steps. Roger and Kevin were riding by on their bikes.

"Where did you go so fast?" demanded Mary Beth. "Why did you leave Tracy's? We were having a good time."

Roger and Kevin came and sat on Molly's steps too.

"I talked with food in my mouth," Molly blurted out.

The three Scouts looked at her.

No one said anything.

She waited for Mary Beth to put her arm around her and say something comforting. She could say, "It will be all right. You can get false teeth. No one will ever find out."

Molly's own grandma had false teeth. They were white and straight and if she didn't take them out at night no one knew they weren't real.

"But why did you leave?" repeated Mary Beth.

"Because my teeth are going to fall out!" Molly screamed. "One is loose already. Remember what Lisa said; 'Talk and chew, no teeth for you'?"

"That's dumb," said Roger. "Talk about dumb."

Then he started to laugh and walk around with his lips over his teeth. Kevin joined him. They both staggered around, laughing on the front lawn.

"You don't really believe that stuff of Lisa's, do you?" asked Mary Beth.

Molly nodded and sobbed and wiped her nose with a piece of Kleenex.

"That's just an old wives' tale," said Mary Beth.

Molly shook her head. "That boy on the playground. The one who was the cheese. He has no teeth."

"Ho, Timmy Johnson," said Kevin. "He just lost his front baby teeth, and the new ones aren't in yet."

Could Molly have missed seeing Timmy

Johnson's molars? Did she just *think* they were missing?

"Look," said Molly, wiggling her loose tooth.

Mary Beth nodded. "It's a baby tooth," she said.

Now Molly felt foolish. Why was she the only one who believed Lisa? Molly always believed people. Especially parents. Parents weren't supposed to lie.

"It's not like a lie," said Mary Beth, as if she were reading Molly's mind. "It's more like a fairy tale."

What a baby Molly had been! Probably even Sonny hadn't believed Lisa.

"It's an easy mistake," said Mary Beth. "Anybody could have been fooled," she said kindly.

Molly felt embarrassed. But she also felt relieved. She wouldn't be fooled so easily again. She wouldn't believe everything she heard.

After the Scouts went home, Molly told her mother about Lisa's rhymes. "Why do people say that if it isn't true?" she asked.

"To help people remember," said her mother. "When you hear a verse like that, it helps you remember not to chew with your mouth full. It's just a trick to help you.

"Remember how you learned, 'When two vowels go walking, the first one does the talking'?"

Molly nodded.

"That helps you know how to pronounce a word when you are reading," she said.

"Well, it works," said Molly. "I'll never talk with my mouth full for my whole life. Even if I'm one hundred!"

CHAPTER 6

The Mock Wedding

The days went by quickly. The Pee Wees wrote down lots of good manners.

At their Tuesday meeting, Roger waved his hand and called, "Don't talk out loud in movies."

"Don't wipe your nose with your sleeve," said Tim.

"He does that. I've seen him," whispered Tracy.

"When I cough, I cover my mouth," said Rachel. "So I don't spread germs."

"I don't have germs," said Sonny.

45

"Everybody has germs, dummy," said Kevin.

"My mom says it's bad manners to talk in church," said Lisa.

Molly wasn't going to pay any attention to anything Lisa's mother said. Lisa's mother was a troublemaker.

When no one else had any more good manners to report, Mrs. Peters said, "We will have lots of wedding talk today. It's time to think about wedding manners. And when we finish, I have a surprise."

The boys groaned. The girls jumped up and down in excitement. They liked weddings. It was fun for Molly to think about brides and long white dresses and cakes with rosebuds on them. And love.

"I hate all that mushy stuff," said Roger.

Rachel cheered. "It's so romantic," she said. "Where is the reception, Mrs. Peters?" she asked.

Rachel knows all about weddings, thought Molly.

"The reception will be in the church basement," said Mrs. Peters.

Mrs. Peters talked about the reception.

She told them it was a party after the wedding. There would be wedding cake. And sandwiches. And punch and soda pop. And little candies and nuts.

"Take out your manners diaries," said Mrs. Peters, "and write down, 'Don't load your plate with food. Take only one sandwich, a few nuts, and a small piece of cake.'"

The Pee Wees wrote it down. They also wrote down, "Don't whisper during the ceremony. Don't kick the church pews. Don't wiggle. Remember all of our good manners on the day of the wedding."

"My mom's got a long dress," said Sonny. "And Larry's got a new suit. I get to carry the wedding ring on a little pillow."

Sonny's lucky, thought Molly. She wished her mother were getting married.

"Moms should get married after they have kids," she said to Mary Beth. "Then the kids could be at the wedding. Sonny's lucky."

Mary Beth looked shocked. "You have to get married first to have kids," she said.

"Do not," said Lisa. "Lots of parents aren't married."

Mrs. Peters clapped her hands. "Some are," she said, "and some are not. And now I have a surprise for you. We are going to the church to practice for the wedding. In fact, we are going to have a little wedding of our own today. A mock wedding!"

Mrs. Peters went on to explain that a mock wedding wasn't a real wedding. It was a pretend wedding.

"Who will be the pretend bride and groom, Mrs. Peters?" asked Rachel.

"Just wait and see," said their leader.

The Scouts all piled into Mrs. Peters's van. Even baby Nick.

When they got to the church, Mrs. Betz was waiting for them.

"Look at that diamond!" whispered Tracy.

"It's huge," said Patty.

"That's the kind I want when I get engaged," said Rachel.

Molly watched the ring sparkle. Every time Mrs. Betz moved her hand, it flashed. She couldn't wait till she was old enough to be married. But who would she marry?

Molly looked around the group. Not Roger. He was a bully. Sonny was nice, but he may still be a baby when he grew up. Kevin had given her a valentine. And he carried her books home from school once. Kevin would be a good boyfriend. A good person to marry. He wanted to be mayor of their town. And he wanted to be rich. Kevin was probably the best bet. Molly decided she would marry Kevin. But she wouldn't tell him yet. It would be her own little secret.

Mrs. Betz explained that on the day of the wedding, the Pee Wees would come down the aisle two by two. Terry, the flower girl, would follow them. She was Sonny's little cousin. She was three. Then Sonny would come in, with the ring on the pillow. And then the bride would walk down the aisle.

"You will all be carrying flowers," she said, "and dropping the petals in the aisle as you walk."

Mrs. Peters showed the Scouts how to walk two by two to the front and stand along the side of the aisle.

"When the ceremony is over, we will walk out the same way and go downstairs to the reception," she added.

"To the food!" said Roger.

Rachel was waving her hand. "Mrs. Peters!" she called. "Will we scatter petals on the way out of the church too?"

"That is a good question, Rachel," said Mrs. Peters. "No, only on the way in."

Molly wished she'd asked a question. A good question.

The Scouts went downstairs to see the reception room. They saw where the cake would stand.

"The room will be decorated on Saturday," said Mrs. Betz. "And there will be flowers and music."

"Are there any questions?" asked Mrs. Peters. "Do we all understand what to do on Saturday?"

The Pee Wees nodded.

"Now," said Mrs. Peters, "we'll have our mock wedding. Let's have Patty pretend to be Terry, the flower girl."

Patty began to blush and act shy. She went to stand beside Mrs. Peters. "You will just pretend to be carrying a little basket of flowers," said Mrs. Peters.

"Now, Sonny will be behind her, with the ring," she said.

Sonny stood behind Patty. He pretended to be carrying a little pillow with the ring.

"Behind them will come the bride and groom," added Mrs. Peters.

All of the Pee Wees waved their hands. They all wanted to be the bride and groom.

"Molly," said Mrs. Peters. "You will make a good bride."

Now Molly turned red. She had dreamed about being a bride, but she never thought it would happen. All the boys were whistling and wanting to be her bridegroom. Molly hoped Mrs. Peters would choose Kevin for the part. It would be fun to pretend Kevin was her bridegroom.

Mrs. Peters looked down the row of Scouts. "Roger," she said. "You be the groom today."

Roger! Anyone but Roger, thought

Molly. Of all the people she didn't want for a pretend husband or a real husband, it was Roger!

Roger had a big grin on his face. He came and stood beside Molly.

All the Pee Wees were snickering.

"The groom will stand at the front of the church," said Mrs. Peters. "Waiting for the bride to come down the aisle."

Mrs. Peters and Mrs. Betz lined the Scouts up two by two and started them down the aisle, scattering make-believe flower petals.

Rachel walked with Kevin.

Next came Tracy and Tim.

And Kenny and Mary Beth.

After the Pee Wees, the flower girl and Sonny followed.

"We don't have any real organ music today," said Mrs. Betz. "But we will hum 'Here Comes the Bride,' so you will get in step."

Mrs. Peters and Mrs. Betz hummed. Mrs. Peters put a lacy white scarf from the Lost and Found on Molly's head. She gave her a fold-up umbrella to use as a make-believe bridal bouquet.

Then she gave her a little shove to start her down the aisle.

As Molly moved down the aisle, she started to feel like a real bride. This was a real church! What if she really were getting married? And to Roger, of all people! But there was no minister, and no ring. No one could get married without a ring. Could they?

When Molly got to the front of the church, Mrs. Peters called, "Now, Roger, you step out and take Molly's arm and stand in front of the minister."

Lisa was the minister. She had a piece of paper in her hand.

"Do you take Roger to be your husband?" she asked Molly.

The Pee Wees were snickering in the aisle.

Molly didn't dare say yes. Even if it was pretend.

"You answer, 'I do,'" called Mrs. Peters.

I'm silly, thought Molly. Lisa wasn't a minister, she was a Scout. And there was no ring.

"I do," said Molly.

"Do you take Molly for your wife?" Lisa asked Roger.

"You bet!" shouted Roger.

"Then say, 'With this ring, I thee wed,'" said Lisa.

Roger pretended to put a ring on Molly's finger. A make-believe ring. "Hi, wife!" he said.

"I now pronounce you husband and wife," said Lisa.

Mrs. Peters started humming organ music again, and just as she did, Roger grabbed Molly and kissed her!

Before Molly knew what she was doing, she took her umbrella-bouquet and hit Roger over the head with it.

"Ouch!" yelled Roger. "You aren't supposed to hit your husband on your wedding day!"

Now the Pee Wees were rolling in the aisle, laughing.

"I only hope this doesn't happen at the real wedding!" said Mrs. Betz.

CHAPTER 7

The Real Wedding

Outside, all the boys sang, "Roger's got a wife!"

And Roger said, "What's for dinner, honey?"

Molly was disgusted. "He's the last person I'd marry," she said to Mary Beth and Lisa.

"You were married in a church," said Lisa.

"Ho, ho," said Molly. "There was no ring." But in the back of her mind, this wedding was too close to real, even if it was pretend.

Mrs. Peters waved good-bye and said, "I have called your parents about what you should wear to the wedding. Be sure to remember good manners."

"I am going to have the best manners of anyone at the wedding," said Rachel. "That's because I have good manners naturally. I don't have to work at it."

"Ha," said Roger. "I'll have a lot more good manners than you do. Just wait and see."

"It's not a contest," Mrs. Peters said, laughing. "Let's all just do our best. And let's remember to smile. A smile makes a rainy day a sunny one."

This was another saying that wasn't true, thought Molly. Just smiling did not change the weather. But Molly wanted that badge, and she wanted to have more good manners than anyone else when she got it. She would smile, all right. She would smile a smile bigger than anyone there. And she would watch everything that Rachel did, and do it better.

"Good, better, best," she sang. "Never let it rest. Until your good is better, and your better, best."

That saying was her grandma's. She could believe her grandma.

Saturday grew closer and closer. The Scouts did not have to have new clothes for the wedding. But they had to wear their best clothes. Their Sunday clothes.

"I'm getting new shoes for the wedding," Tracy said one day after school.

"I wonder what Tim is wearing," said Lisa. "He hasn't got a good suit. I'll bet he comes in jeans."

"I heard he's going to wear one of Sonny's suits," said Kenny.

"Sonny's fatter than Tim," said Patty. "It might not fit."

"I'm wearing the dress I wore for my cousin's wedding," said Rachel. "It's organdy."

Molly had an almost-new blue dress with little daisies on it. Her mother said it was just right for a wedding. She had blue shoes to match it.

"My mom's going to curl my hair with her curling iron," Molly told the others.

"I'm going to my mom's hairdresser in the morning," said Rachel. "She's going to style my hair."

It was hard to keep up with Rachel, thought Molly. But she was going to try. Especially with manners. Rachel wasn't going to have one single better manner than she did. No matter what.

When Sonny's mother's wedding day came, it was raining.

"Dear me," said Mrs. Duff. "Our curls will straighten out in the dampness."

"We'll have to run between the drops," said Mr. Duff, who was going to the wedding too.

"We'll take umbrellas," said Molly's mother.

Molly remembered Mrs. Peters's words. "A smile makes a rainy day a sunny one." Molly doubted it. But she'd try.

Molly smiled. Then she ran to the window. It was still raining. She smiled again. She looked outside again. A bolt of lightning flashed in the sky. It didn't work.

As it got closer to two o'clock, Molly got excited.

At one o'clock she had her bath.

At one-fifteen she put her best blue dress on.

At one-thirty she put her new socks and shoes on.

Then her mother combed her hair and put a ribbon in it.

Everyone got into the car. Then they drove to the Kellys' and picked up Mary Beth.

"I've never been to a wedding before," said Mary Beth. "Except the mock wedding."

When they got to the church, the other Pee Wees were running from cars to the front door.

"I'm soaked!" said Tim.

Tim's borrowed suit was wet. It looked a little baggy on him. His hair hung down over his eyes. Mrs. Peters tried to comb his hair back, but it still looked like he'd just come out of the shower.

"What a nasty day!" said Mrs. Peters.

All the Pee Wees moved around, trying to get dry. They straightened their clothes. They fussed with their hair.

Rachel was the last one to arrive. She was wrapped up in a plastic raincoat and her

mother had a huge umbrella over her head.

"She looks like a package," snickered Roger.

But when Rachel was unwrapped, she was bone-dry. Her curls bounced and her dress stood out around her. It didn't hang limp like the others' did.

"I wonder where the bride is," whispered Lisa.

"Look at Sonny!" called Roger.

For the first time ever, Sonny looked grown-up to Molly. He didn't look like a baby. He had on a brown suit, and a white shirt, and a real grown-up tie. The tie looked a little tight. It made Sonny's face red.

Mrs. Peters passed out the peonies. They were pink. She showed the Scouts how to hold them in their left arms, and scatter petals with their right hands.

All of a sudden organ music began to

play. It was starting. The real wedding. Mrs. Betz was going to be Mrs. Stone when it was over.

Mrs. Peters lined the Pee Wees up two by two. They had the same partners as at the mock wedding. Molly's partner was Roger. They were first in line, and as the organ music began, Mrs. Peters gave them a little push to start them down the aisle.

There was a long white runner on the floor. The smell of flowers filled the air. White bows were tied on all the pews. And candles glowed all over the church.

"You look beautiful!" whispered Mrs. Peters to her Scouts.

Pink petals fell onto the white runner. Molly could have cried, it was so romantic. If only she were walking with Kevin instead of Roger.

Sonny followed the other Pee Wees, because he was the ring bearer. He walked behind Terry, the flower girl.

The Pee Wees stood to one side, and the real bride, with her long white dress and veil and flowers, walked up and took Larry's arm. The real wedding was about to begin. Before long, Sonny would have a father!

CHAPTER 8

Roger's Wife

Mrs. Betz looks beautiful, thought Molly. Not like an assistant troop leader at all. And Larry was so handsome. Even more handsome than he was in his fireman's uniform.

The minister stepped forward and smiled.

He gave a little talk. All of a sudden Molly remembered about good manners. She looked at the other Pee Wees. Rachel was smiling as Mrs. Peters had told them to.

Molly smiled a bigger smile than Rachel's.

When Rachel saw her, she smiled bigger than Molly. Molly smiled even bigger than Rachel, and her mouth opened up into a grin.

Rachel leaned over and grinned back.

What could Molly do that was better? What was bigger than a grin?

A laugh. If smiling was good, and grinning was better, then laughing would be best!

Molly laughed out loud. She looked at Rachel. Rachel didn't laugh. Everyone was staring at Molly. And the more they stared, the more Molly laughed.

"Stop it!" whispered Mary Beth from down the aisle.

Even Roger gave her a poke.

But Molly couldn't stop. Her shoulders shook.

Mrs. Peters walked up and tapped Molly on the shoulder and still Molly laughed. Louder and longer. The more she tried to stop laughing, the worse it got. It sounded very noisy in the quiet church.

Now Mrs. Peters was frowning. All of a sudden Molly stopped laughing. She was embarrassed. Laughing must not be better than smiling. It felt awful. Mrs. Peters patted Molly on the shoulder and went back to her place.

The minister was still talking. He said some of the same words that Lisa had at the mock wedding. The Pee Wees watched. Molly heard someone sobbing. She looked around. It was Mary Beth. "It's so beautiful," she whispered, tears in her eyes.

"Do you take this man as your lawful wedded husband?" asked the minister.

"I do," said Mrs. Betz.

Larry turned around for the ring. Sonny handed it to him.

Just at that moment, Roger reached into his pocket. He took something out. A little silver ring from a gum machine.

"With this ring, I thee wed," Larry repeated after the minister.

Roger whispered the words with Larry.

Before Molly knew what was happening, Roger grabbed her hand and pushed the ring on her fourth finger. As he did, the minister announced in a loud voice, "I now pronounce you husband and wife."

"We're married!" shouted Roger, as the organ played heavy chords in the background.

Oh, no! Was Roger right?

A real church.

A real minister.

A real ring on Molly's finger.

Was Molly really married to Roger White?

Up the aisle they went, with everyone cheering the bride and groom.

"Meet Mrs. White!" said Roger when they got to the back of the church and stood in the reception line.

Molly stuck her tongue out at Roger.

"Ho, ho," said Roger. "Mrs. Peters,

Molly stuck out her tongue in church—bad manners, bad manners!"

Molly felt like crying. Now she had another bad manner at the wedding, and this one was all Roger's fault. On top of the bad manners, she might be married to Roger for life!

"Downstairs!" called Mrs. Peters. "Time for the reception."

As the Pee Wees started down the steps, Molly looked outside.

It had stopped raining.

The sun was out. Maybe smiling did work after all. If it did, it was because of Molly. Surely no one ever tried harder to smile than she had today.

"Look!" shouted Patty, when they got downstairs. "It's beautiful!"

Patty was right. The room did not look like the place they had seen earlier. There were balloons and flowers and ferns. And white tablecloths and streamers and candles everywhere.

But Molly couldn't enjoy the reception. She was embarrassed about the laughing. She was embarrassed about Roger. And what if she was married to Roger? For the rest of her life!

"Sonny Stone," said Roger, clapping Sonny on the back. "Hey, that's his name now. We can call him Stoney for short."

"Or Rocky," said Kenny, laughing at his own joke.

"Line up," said Mrs. Peters to the Pee Wees. "Line up for pictures."

The photographer set his camera on a little stand. He told the Pee Wees to smile.

Roger whispered to Molly, "Smile, Mrs. White!"

Click, click, click.

Was this Molly's wedding picture too?

The photographer took a picture of Sonny's parents. And Sonny and his parents. Then the bride and groom and grandparents.

"Time to cut the cake," called one of the church ladies.

Everyone followed the bride and groom to a little table with a big cake on it.

"It's four stories high!" shouted Sonny.

Everyone snickered.

"Those are tiers," said Rachel. On top of the cake was a little plastic bride and groom.

"They don't look like Mrs. Stone and Larry," whispered Mary Beth.

"But it's romantic," said Lisa.

The photographer set up his camera in front of the cake. Mrs. Stone picked up a silver knife with a white bow on it. She and Larry smiled as she sliced right through the middle of a pink rosebud made of frosting.

Click, went the camera. Click, click.

After that, the Pee Wees each took a paper plate with a silver bell on it. Each napkin said "Louise and Larry" in the corner.

The Scouts filled their plates with little sandwiches and candies and mints with nuts and wedding cake. Molly took just enough. And not too much. She would not add another bad manner to the list. Or another worry.

The Pee Wees sat down at one of the long tables with white streamers and flowers in the middle. They all remembered not to talk while they chewed their food.

Sonny went back for more food when his was gone.

How can Sonny eat, Molly wondered. A wedding and a new father all in one day.

"Why were you laughing in church?" Tracy asked Molly. "What was so funny about a wedding?"

"I was smiling," said Molly.

"It was a pretty loud smile," said Kevin. "It's bad manners to laugh in church."

Molly tried to explain what happened. "I tried to smile more than Rachel. And it turned into a laugh."

"That happened to me once, when I was

little," said Mrs. Peters. "I went to church with a friend of mine and she said something funny and I laughed. Once I started I couldn't stop. The more I tried to stop, the more I laughed. It was awful. I know just how Molly felt."

"That's just what happened!" cried Molly, in surprise. "I couldn't stop, but I wanted to."

Mrs. Peters put her arm around Molly. "Some things we just can't help," she added.

Molly was surprised to hear that Mrs. Peters had laughed out loud in church. A Scout leader with bad manners! Molly felt a little better now. Her own mother couldn't get cross with her when they got home, if she heard Mrs. Peters had done the same thing.

"What did Roger put on your finger?" whispered Mary Beth.

Molly pulled Roger's ring off her finger
and threw it into a potted plant. Not that it
would make any difference now. The dam-
age was done.

"I'm married to him!" cried Molly. She had to tell someone.

"It was only a mock wedding," said Mary Beth. "It wasn't real."

Molly shook her head. "Today it was a real wedding. He put a ring on my finger when the minister said 'I now pronounce you husband and wife.' He called me Mrs. White!"

Now some of the other Pee Wees gathered around Molly and Mary Beth.

"Roger hates mushy stuff," said Tracy. "Why would he want to marry you?"

"To make me mad," said Molly, stomping her foot. "I hate him!"

"Well, you're not really married," said Rachel. "That's dumb."

"She might be," said Lisa. "It's in church and everything."

"Do you have a license?" demanded Rachel. "A marriage license?"

Everyone looked at Rachel. They knew about a car license. And a dog license. Even a bike license. But no one knew about a license to get married.

"Do Larry and Mrs. Stone have a license?" asked Mary Beth.

"Of course," said Rachel. "It's not legal if you don't get one at the courthouse."

Molly could have hugged Rachel. Rachel knew a lot. And sometimes it paid off.

"You're off the hook," Rachel said. "But I wouldn't fool around with stuff like that."

"I won't," said Molly in relief. "I'm not getting near Roger again."

Waiters came around with little trays of cookies. And little dishes of ice cream. This time Molly ate some. She was hungry now. And happy. Roger was putting peanuts down Patty Baker's neck. It looked like he had forgotten the whole Mrs. White business already.

"This is as good as a birthday party," said Tim.

"It's better," said Kevin. "We don't have to play those games, like Pin the Tail on the Donkey."

It was a good party, thought Molly. Everyone was happy and laughing. The food tasted good. And it was fun to see Sonny get a new father.

"I'm going to have a satin wedding gown when I get married," said Lisa. "A real long one, with a huge, long veil."

"Me too," said Mary Beth.

Molly wasn't going to think about weddings or gowns. Not for a long, long time.

When all the food was gone, and all the pictures were taken, Larry and Mrs. Stone got ready to leave.

"They are going on their honeymoon," whispered Mary Beth.

"Is Sonny going too?" asked Tim.

"Kids don't go on honeymoons," said Rachel in disgust. "Honeymoons are for romance. Who would want Sonny around if you wanted to be romantic?"

"She's going to throw her bouquet!" shouted Lisa. "The one who catches it is the next one married. My mom told me."

Mrs. Stone was waving now, from the doorway. She lifted her bouquet of flowers and got ready to throw it. Everyone scrambled around trying to get close.

The bouquet tumbled through the air, right straight toward Molly. Everyone else reached for it, but it fell right into Molly's hands! Plop! Oh no!

It didn't matter. It would be years and years away. And when she really did get married, she would marry Kevin. He would be mayor and maybe even president. She watched him explaining to Sonny how a camera worked. He didn't know

Molly's secret—yet. It was too soon to tell him. Molly would keep this a secret for a long, long time. She wouldn't tell him until they were both grown-up. And she would get the license herself.

As everyone got ready to leave, Mrs. Peters said, "Don't forget our meeting next Tuesday. We have some badges to give out to everyone!"

"I'll be there," said Molly.

Good manners were a lot of work. But it was worth it. Never in her whole life would she talk with food in her mouth. Or laugh out loud in church.

Especially at a wedding.

♪ ♪ ♪ **Pee Wee Scout Song** ♪ ♪ ♪

(to the tune of
"Old MacDonald Had a Farm")

Scouts are helpers, Scouts have fun
Pee Wee, Pee Wee Scouts!
We sing and play when work is done,
Pee Wee, Pee Wee Scouts!

With a good deed here,
And an errand there,
Here a hand, there a hand,
Everywhere a good hand.

Scouts are helpers, Scouts have fun,
Pee Wee, Pee Wee Scouts!

Pee Wee Scout Pledge

We love our country
And our home,
Our school and neighbors too.

As Pee Wee Scouts
We pledge our best
In everything we do.